Jazz Accordion Solos

by Gary Dahl

Online Audio   www.melbay.com/96309MEB

Audio Contents

1. Poor Butterfly [2:15]
2. After You've Gone [2:37]
3. Peg O' My Heart [1:33]
4. Avalon [1:59]
5. A Good Man is Hard to Find [2:38]
6. Swanee [1:51]
7. Indiana [2:32]
8. The Japanese Sandman [2:03]
9. You Made Me Love You [2:06]
10. Alexander's Ragtime Band [2:18]

1 2 3 4 5 6 7 8 9 0

© 1997 BY MEL BAY PUBLICATIONS, INC., PACIFIC, MO 63069.
ALL RIGHTS RESERVED. INTERNATIONAL COPYRIGHT SECURED. B.M.I. MADE AND PRINTED IN U.S.A.

Visit us on the Web at http://www.melbay.com — E-mail us at email@melbay.com

⇥ CONTENTS ⇤

⇥ ABOUT THE AUTHOR ⇤

Gary Dahl is currently active as an accordionist, composer, arranger, and educator residing in Puyallup, Washington. He is certified by the American Accordionist's Association, Northwest Accordion Teachers Association, and received a BA degree from the University of Washington with a minor in music theory/harmony. Since 1960, Mr. Dahl's students have been consistent winners in National/State competitions and many have achieved professional status. The Gary Dahl Trio plus vocalist perform regularly at private clubs, hotels, and lounges. Mr. Dahl studied with Joe Spano and continues his productive teaching philosophy.

⇥ FOREWORD ⇤

The arranging goal was to bridge the gap from classical and/or traditional "Lady of Spain" accordion solos to professional jazz-styled solos. Chord symbols are included with each arrangement to facilitate study of harmony and analysis. Not every passing chord is notated; e.g.: a dominant seventh chord may be written as a G7 even though the melody passes through the ninth, flatted ninth, raised ninth, eleventh, raised eleventh (written often as a flatted fifth to ease understanding), or thirteenth. A typical G9(13) chord will occasionally be written only as a G9 to eliminate clutter. The recording accompanying this book follows the music as written but with added rhythm, rubato, and slight improvisation. The player is encouraged to add extra rhythmic and improvisational ideas.

Additional Arranging Goals:
- Music that is fun to play and enjoyable to listen to;
- Music with a sensible degree of difficulty, such that any additional difficulty would not improve the sound of the overall arrangement;
- Music that utilizes the orchestral capabilities of the accordion;
- Including sufficient musicality to satisfy the professional;
- Harmony that is creative and expressive but will not alienate the audience at large;
- Music with a logical harmonic flow – not haphazard or disjunct;
- Music that will excite and challenge intermediate through professional players, aided and inspired by the recording;
- Music that is in the Public Domain (out of copyright), used to keep the price reasonable. This music was written between 1913 and the early 1920s. It represents a golden era of popular music.

"Dear Gary: Thanks for sending your new book, Jazz Accordion Solos. It is excellent material for the intermediate through professional. Accordionists need this type of book to introduce them to jazz styles. [This book is] especially for the accordionist who has only played the traditional accordion music and would like to make the transition from classical and polka to jazz. The arrangements are very musical and well-written. Thanks again and good luck to you and Mel Bay Publications, Inc."

. . . Frank Marocco

"Gary Dahl has created a finely-tuned collection of solo arrangements for the jazz accordion enthusiast. As an arranger, he fully utilizes the accordion's orchestral and rhythmic qualities, combining well-balanced sonorities between both hands . . . Good for study purposes as well as solo performance."

. . . Nick Ariondo

"Dear Gary: Thanks for sending the charts; they sound very good and should be a challenging test for most 'box' players. I got a kick out of some of your fingerings which is necessary for the occasional awkward jazz passage. Good luck with the book; Mel Bay should be happy with it. Keep Swingin'!"

. . . Art Van Damme

→ POOR BUTTERFLY ←

Music by John Golden © 1916
Arr. by Gary Dahl for
Mel Bay Pub., Inc. 1/1/96

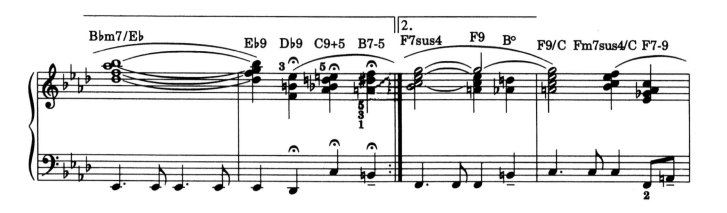

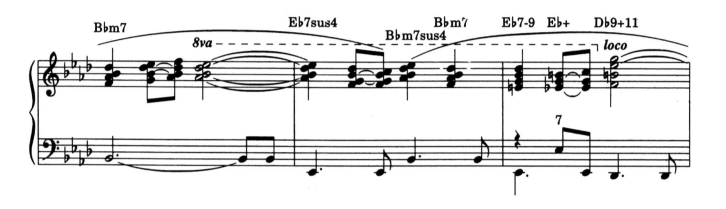

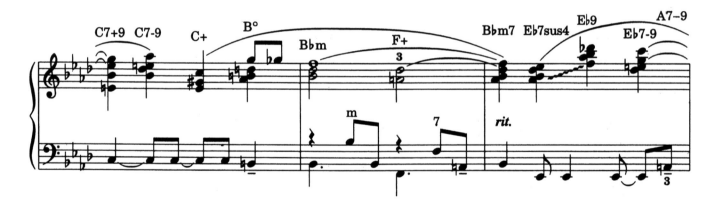

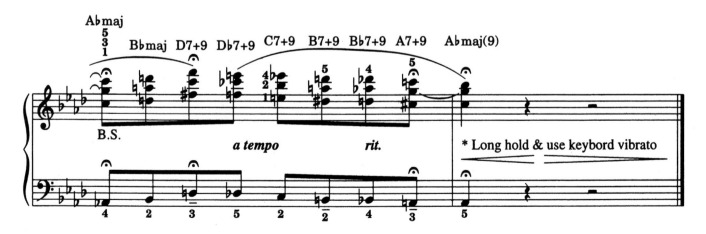

⇥ AFTER YOU'VE GONE ⇤

Music by Turner Layton © 1918
Arr. by Gary Dahl for
Mel Bay Pub., Inc. 11/20/95

Play 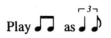 as

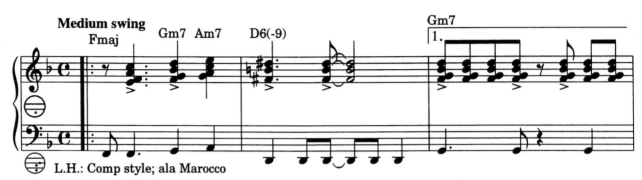

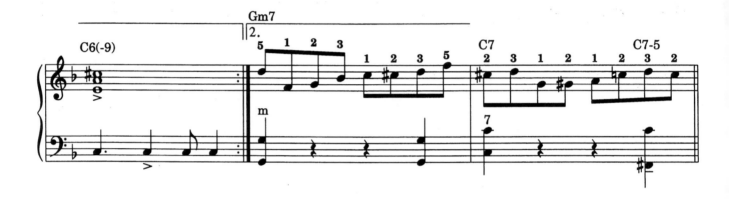

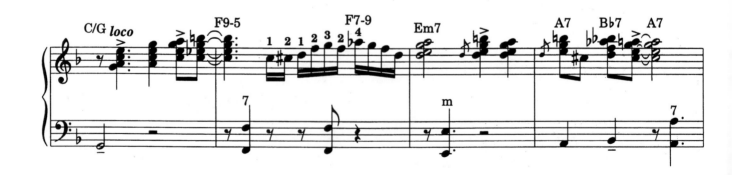

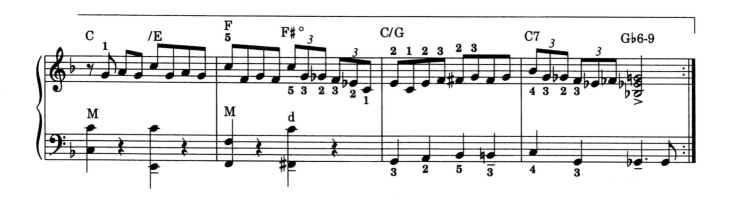

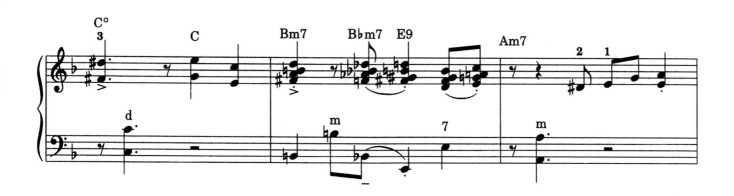

10

→PEG O' MY HEART←

Music by Fred Fisher © 1913
Arr. by Gary Dahl for
Mel Bay Pub., Inc. 10/17/95

① Long bass notes but not slurred.

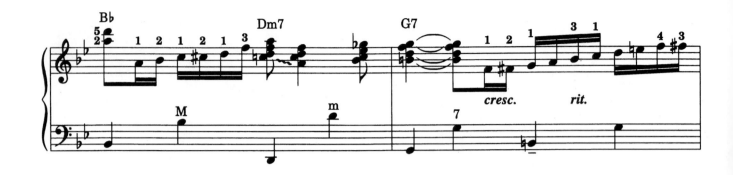

Slower... bluesy

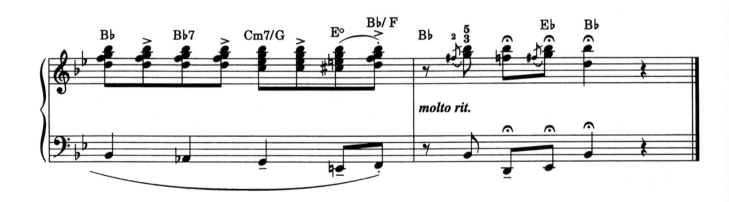

AVALON

Music by Vincent Rose © 1920
Arr. by Gary Dahl for
Mel Bay Pub., Inc. 12/9/95

Play all ♩♩ as ♩♪

* 2nd time: Use your own ad lib. variations.

E.G. ① Play some chords as
② Change time patterns

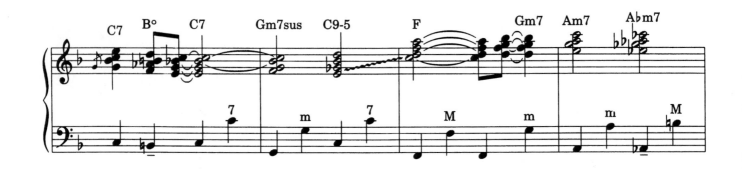

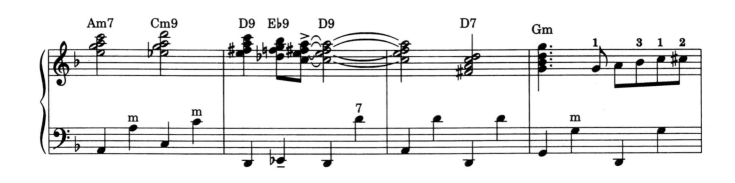

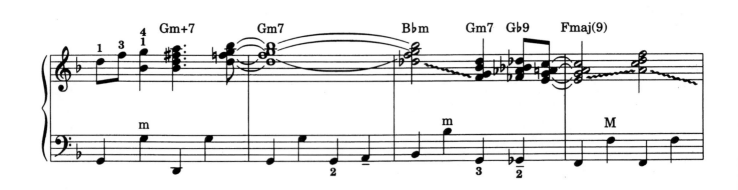

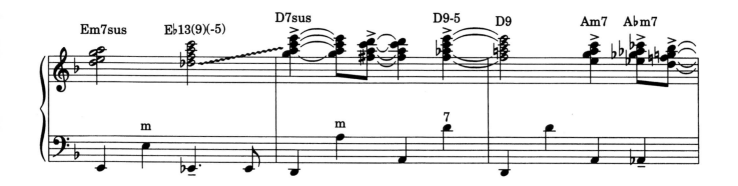

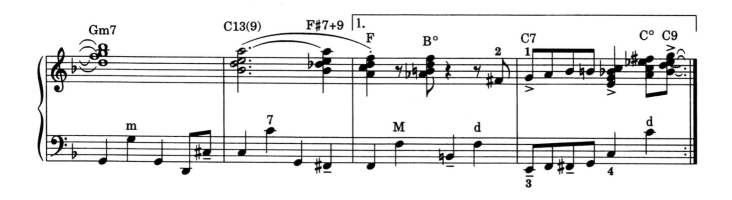

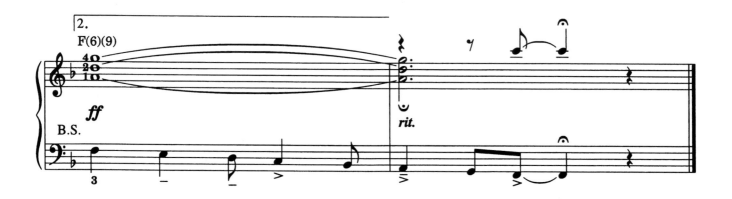

⇢ A GOOD MAN IS HARD TO FIND ⇠

Music by Eddle Green © 1916
Arr. by Gary Dahl for
Mel Bay Pub., Inc. 11/24/95

*2nd time: L.H. ♩ ♩ / R.H. all ♩ ♩ in * measures

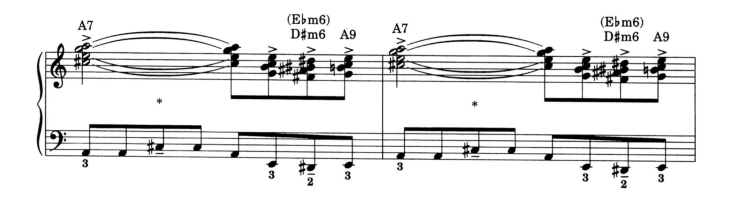

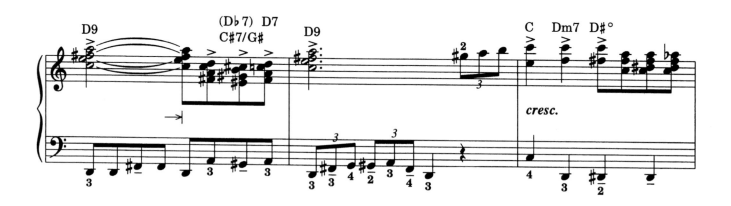

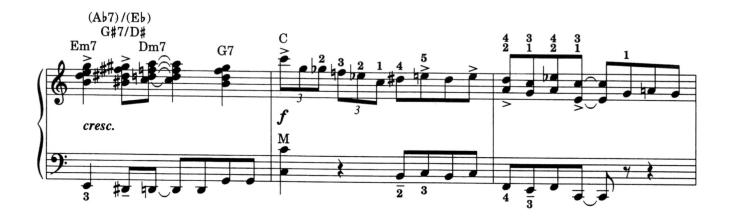

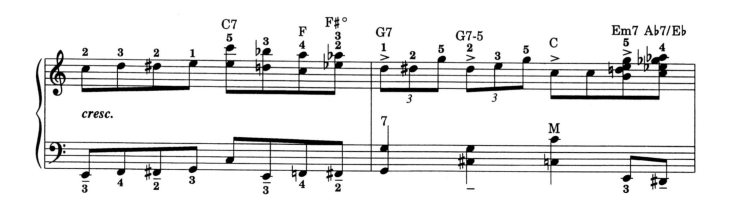

19

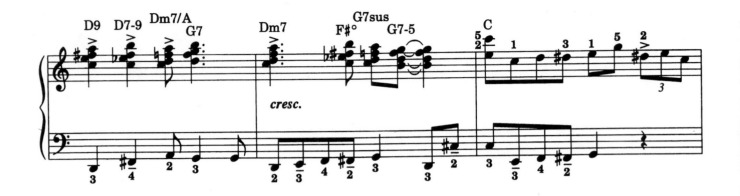

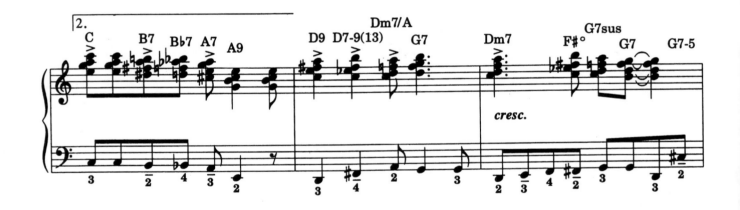

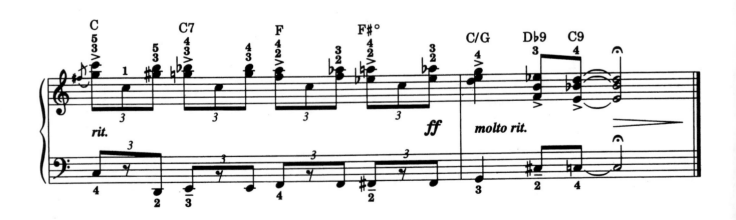

SWANEE

Music by George Gershwin© 1919
Arr. by Gary Dahl for
Mel Bay Pub., Inc. 2/24/96

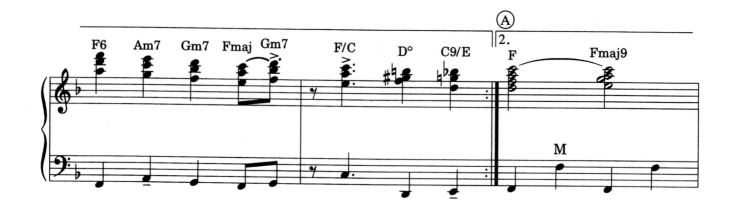

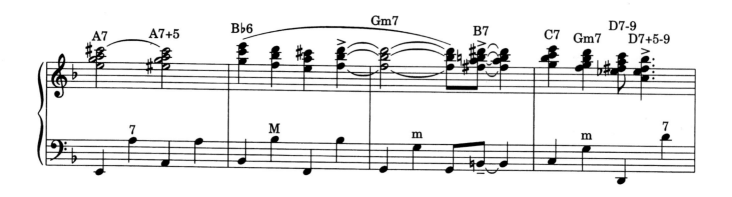

→ INDIANA ←
(Back home again in)

Music by James Hanley © 1917
Arr. by Gary Dahl for
Mel Bay Pub., Inc. 5/15/96

26

27

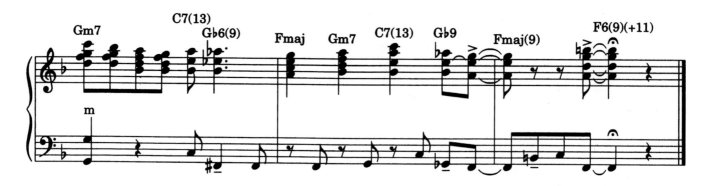

THE JAPANESE SANDMAN

Music by Richard Whiting © 1920
Arr. by Gary Dahl for
Mel Bay Pub., Inc. 3/16/96

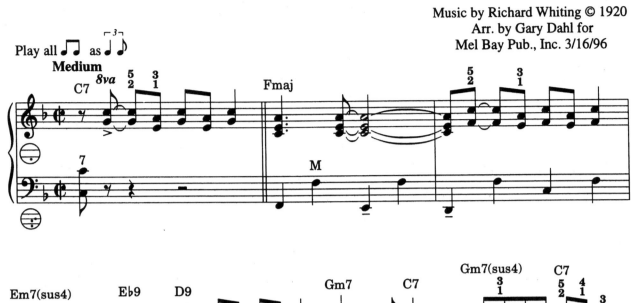

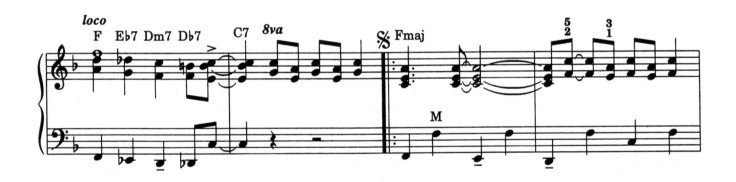

⇢ YOU MADE ME LOVE YOU ⇠

Music by James Monaco © 1913
Arr. by Gary Dahl for
Mel Bay Pub., Inc. 3/30/96

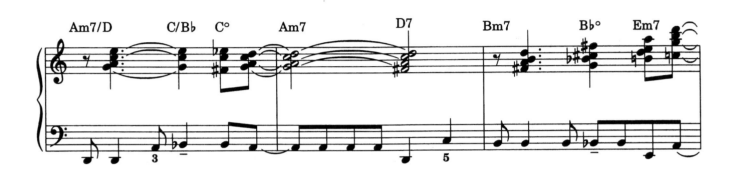

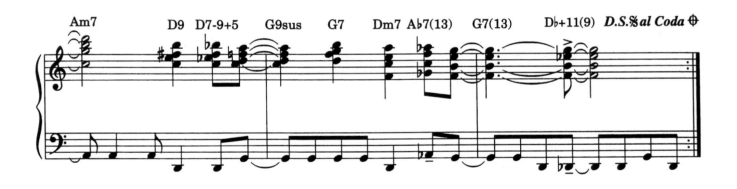

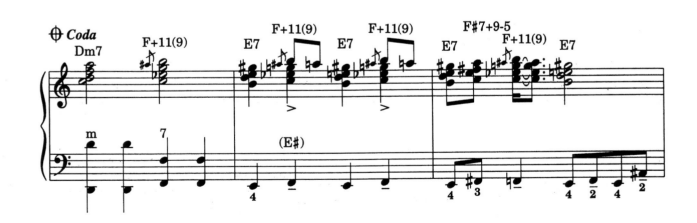

33

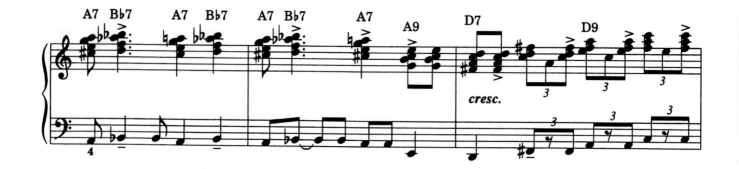

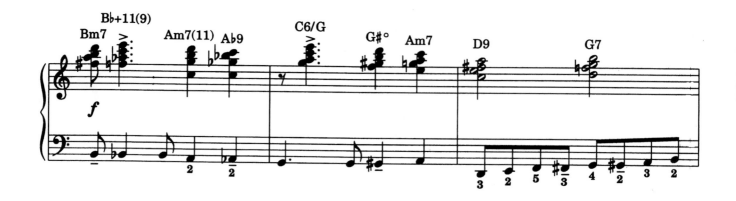

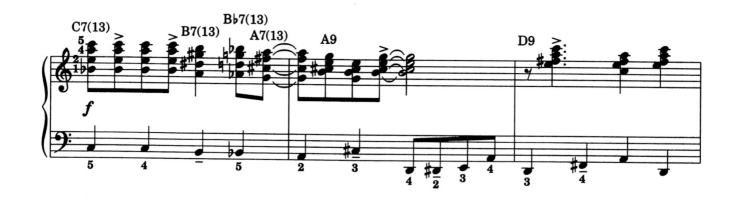

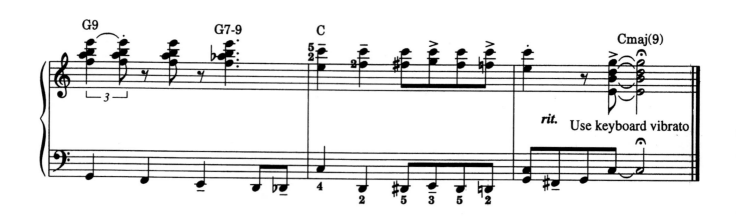

This page has been left blank to avoid awkward page turns

ALEXANDER'S RAGTIME BAND

Music by Irving Berlin © 1916
Arr. by Gary Dahl for
Mel Bay Pub., Inc. 3/5/96

Play all ♫ as ♩♪

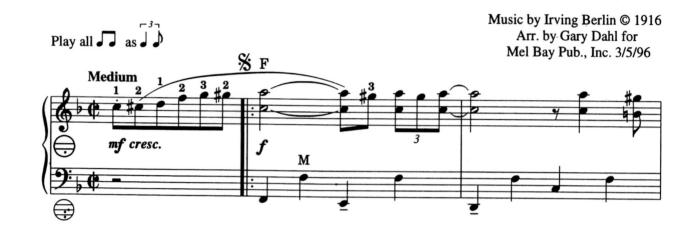

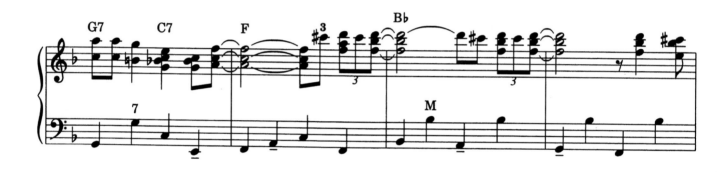

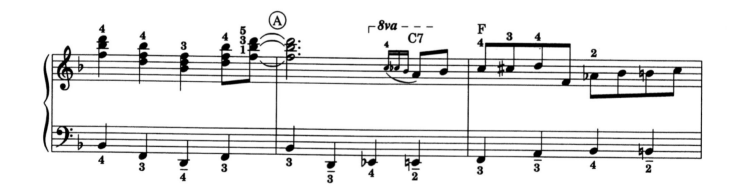

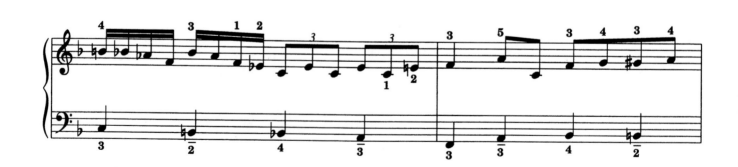

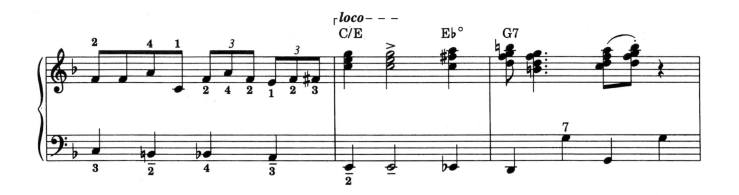

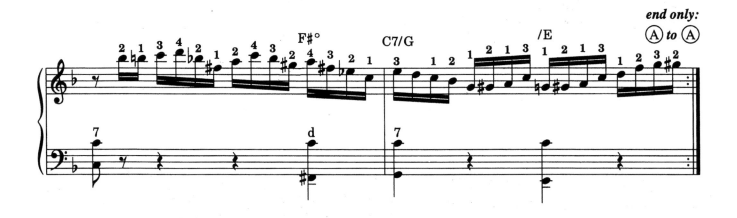

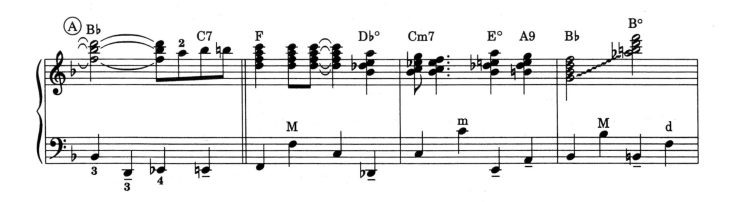

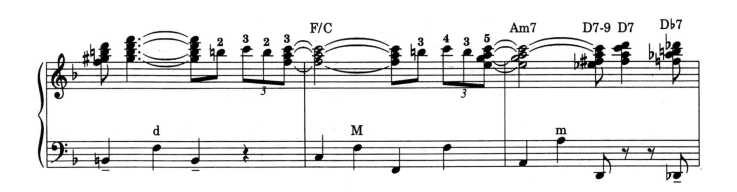

Great Music at Your Fingertips